A MYSTERIOUS CASE OF BOOKS, BARKS & BURGLARY

CURLY BAY ANIMAL RESCUE COZY MYSTERY BOOK 9

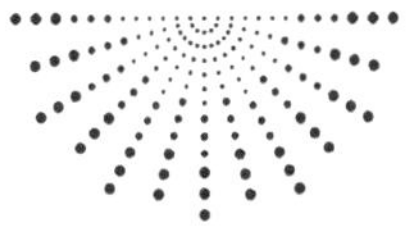

DONNA DOYLE

PUREREAD.COM

CONTENTS

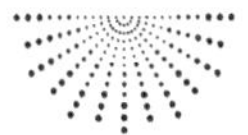

Courtney Cain sat at her desk at the Curly Bay Pet Hotel and Rescue, frowning at her phone. She plugged it in to the charger she usually kept nearby for emergencies, but the little symbol to show it was working wouldn't come up on the screen. Courtney unplugged it, plugged it back in again, and frowned even deeper when it still wouldn't work.

"What's the matter?" Jessi asked as she walked in from the shelter side. She plopped a leash down on her desk and ran a hand through her short hair. Jessi was a fan of big, dangly earrings, and the ones she wore today were glittery snowflakes on little chains that dusted her shoulders. "Are the books not adding up?"

"Huh? Oh." Courtney realized she had the spreadsheet for the shelter's finances open on her computer. She'd gotten so distracted by her phone that she'd forgotten what she'd been doing in the first place. "No, all that is fine. I'm just frustrated with this phone. It was working just fine until about a week ago. Now it doesn't want to take a charge, or it takes forever to charge. Yesterday it died on me completely, and I swear the battery was at forty percent at least."

"Try restarting it," Jessi suggested. "I've done that sometimes before when it's being a little picky."

"I'll give it a shot." Courtney held in the power button and watched the screen begin to cycle through whatever magical little processes it did to restart. "I really don't want to have to pay for a new one."

"Well, you might want to," Jessi advised as she rummaged around in her desk drawer and found a candy bar. "They're saying it's going to be a really bad winter this year. You don't want to be stranded without a cell phone."

"I have a hard time believing we'd even get a flake of snow, considering it's barely cold enough out to wear a sweater," Courtney noted. They'd had a few chilly days, but the winter thus far had mostly just been rainy.

Jessi shook her head, sending her earrings shimmering once again. "It's better to be safe than sorry. Our winters are pretty mild, but every now and then it feels like we're on the edge of the Arctic."

"I second that," Dora said as she came into the office, brushing off a few stray dog hair clippings from her shirt. Dora was in charge of the pet hotel and day spa side of the business, and it was this work that helped them fund all the strays they took into the shelter. She sometimes came across as a little crabby, but that was just because she preferred dogs and cats to people. "All the old men are saying the elements are just right, and we're going to get some really nasty weather. I hope you've stocked up."

"Stocked up?" Courtney asked. "Surely even if it gets bad, I can still get to the grocery store."

Dora sat down, took off her glasses, and wiped them on the inside hem of her shirt. "You were living in the city before you came here," she reminded Courtney. "You were probably within walking distance of anything that you desperately needed, and the snowplow would make it by within a few hours anyway, right?"

"Right," Courtney affirmed. She'd seen a few bad winters, but it'd never been anything she couldn't handle. "No big deal."

The older woman laughed softly as she shook her head. "Curly Bay has some pretty limited resources when it comes to snowplows and the like. They only have one, I believe, and it takes quite some time just for it to do the main routes, much less all the side roads. When the weather even thinks about getting nasty, the schools close up instead of trying to get the roads cleared."

"I didn't realize," Courtney admitted. She'd always just imagined that any city would pull all the machinery out of the garage and get the job done, but Curly Bay was a pretty small town.

"And you're not thinking about how far out of town you live now," Dora added. "How are you going to get down your driveway if we get six or ten inches of snow, much less that rural road?"

A wave of anxiety washed over Courtney. "I didn't think of any of that. I guess I'll have to get to the store. My new kitchen has a wonderful pantry, but I've always felt it's pretty wasted with just me living there. I think the most it has in it is a few cans of soup."

"My parents live like the apocalypse is coming," Jessi said with a fond smile as she polished off her candy bar. "They've got a little bomb shelter just full of bottled water and canned goods. We've almost never needed it, but it makes them feel better."

Stocking up was definitely going on her To Do list, but Courtney had a new worry in mind. "What about the shelter? The animals will need to be taken care of no matter what happens to the roads."

"My house is just a couple blocks from here," Dora reassured her, "and my brother has a four-wheel-drive truck. I can get here almost no matter what, so we should be good on that."

"Thank goodness." Courtney checked her phone, seeing that it was now charging. "You guys were really getting me scared there for a minute."

Jessi leaned over to toss her wrapper in the trash. "I'm sorry. I didn't mean to do that. I just hate hearing stories of people who are stuck and don't have any supplies. You can blame that on my parents, I guess. They're the definition of prepared."

The phone rang just then, and Jessi snagged it off her desk. "Curly Bay Pet Hotel and Rescue. This is Jessi. How can I help you?" Her brows creased and her face sagged a little as she listened. "Yes, she's right here. Just a moment. Courtney, it's for you. It's Miles Dorrington, and he sounds upset."

Courtney picked up the extension on her desk. It was rare that they had anyone upset at them. Courtney might be the manager, but with women like Jessi and Dora at her side, operations were usually pretty smooth. They knew how to work together despite their differences, and they hadn't really had any complaints. "Hi, Mr. Dorrington. This is Courtney. What can I do for you this afternoon?"

"You can take my next appointment off your books!" the older man bellowed over the phone.

Flicking over to the schedule on her computer, Courtney searched for Mr. Dorrington's name. "All right. I see we have you set for next Wednesday. Did you need me to move that to a different day?" She forced herself to smile so she would sound friendly over the phone. No matter what his problem was, Courtney didn't want anyone to claim she'd been anything less than professional.

"No!" Miles barked. His own dog was barking in the background. "I don't want to come in at all! Never again!"

"Is there a problem?" Courtney pressed.

"As if you have to ask!" he retorted. "I should take a picture of my Lulabelle and have my granddaughter post it all over the internet! It's atrocious!"

Courtney pressed her lips together to keep herself from giggling at the idea of him using his granddaughter to bash them online. It was a serious situation, though, and she sobered quickly. "I'm afraid I really don't understand what's wrong, Mr. Dorrington. Could you explain it to me?"

An irritated huff came over the line. "I brought Lulabelle in for her normal grooming session, and Dora cut her hair far too short! The poor thing is going to freeze to death! Fortunately, I already had some sweaters for her just for fun, but she'll have to wear them for at least a month while this terrible haircut grows out!"

"Could I put you on hold for just a moment?" Courtney made sure she was on mute before she turned to Dora, who was watching her with anticipation. "Was there a problem with Lulabelle when Mr. Dorrington brought her in last?"

She raised her dark eyebrows. "Everything was business as usual. Bath, blow-dry, cut, nail trim, a little polish, and a bow in her hair. It's the same thing she's been having done for the last few years."

"He didn't say anything about it being too short?" Courtney pressed. She had no reason to doubt Dora, but this was very unusual.

"Not a thing," the groomer affirmed, looking mystified and offended.

"Mr. Dorrington?" Courtney said when she returned to the line. "I don't see anything in my records that anything was done differently than normal. However, it's our policy to make sure the customer is happy. Perhaps there's something I can do to make it up to you? A free grooming session?"

"Absolutely not! Then she'll just butcher my sweet Lulabelle the rest of the way! I can't imagine what the poor girl would do if she came home completely bald the next time. No. You're never getting my business again." The line went dead.

Courtney sucked in a deep breath as she put the phone back. "Well, there goes one of our highest-paying patrons."

"Honestly, Courtney. I did everything just the way I always do," Dora said apologetically. "I can double-check my notes if you'd like."

"No, that's not necessary," Courtney replied quickly. "I know you do a good job, Dora. I doubt this is your fault at all. Maybe it was a communication error or something, I don't know." She pressed her knuckles against her chin as she rested her elbow on the desk, trying to think.

"If I'm honest, I'm kind of glad he didn't take you up on your offer of a free grooming session," Jessi piped up. "I mean, he's one of the wealthiest people in Curly Bay. He can afford it."

"Yes," Courtney agreed, "but that also means he can afford to take his business anywhere he wants to, even if he has to go over Ruby Cove or even further. Our funding is really important, and I hate to lose him. Still, if he's going to be like that, then maybe we're better off without him."

Dora shook her head. "I know I shouldn't take it personally, but this is frustrating. I'm tempted to call him back and ask him to bring her in just so I can see what he's talking about."

"Give him some time to calm down," Courtney advised. "I'll try to give him a call next week and see if I can work it out with him."

"All right. Well, I guess I'm going to get back to my appointments. I've got a Schnauzer who'll appreciate a trim. I hope." She turned and headed back toward the grooming salon, muttering to herself.

Courtney could understand her frustration. She glanced at her phone, seeing that at least it was charging now.

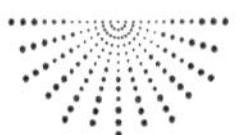

"That's a good girl," Courtney crooned from the driver's seat to the golden retriever sitting next to her. "You like car rides, don't you? You're going to get a home so fast you won't know what's happening. It'll definitely happen after today." She smiled and ruffled the dog's ears.

When they reached the library, Lisa met them at the door. Lisa and Courtney had quickly become friends, both having moved to Curly Bay at around the same time. She had half of her short, curly hair pulled up and secured with a barrette. "Oh, Courtney! You're right! She looks just like her!" Lisa held the door open to let the two of them in, and then they began making their way to the children's room. "As soon as I told our regular group that we'd be having a special guest this week, they were begging their parents to make sure they could come back. I think a few of them have brought their friends as well, considering how many kids are already in here. You think Shelby will do well with the crowd?"

"I'm certain of it," Courtney replied. "A lot of shelter dogs have a lot of trouble adjusting to new places and new people, but I swear she gets a kick out of it."

She was soon proven correct when they entered the children's room. Dozens of wide eyes turned to stare, and then all the screams and excitement began over seeing a big fluffy dog at the library. Shelby wagged her tail and eagerly sniffed at the legs of the nearest child, who squealed in delight.

"All right, boys and girls!" Lisa said loudly, holding up her hand to signal to the children that they needed to quiet down. "Today, we have Miss Courtney from the Curly Bay Pet Hotel and Rescue. She's brought Shelby with her. I know you're all very excited to meet Shelby, and I promise each and every one of you will get a chance to pet her. First, let's get to our story." She handed a book to Courtney.

The cover featured a dog just like Shelby, which made this an absolutely perfect opportunity. Courtney read aloud while Shelby sat patiently next to her. She knew the kids were probably far more focused on the dog than on the story, but she didn't mind. There was a certain little thrill to making this whole room of kids so happy. Lisa had done an excellent job picking out the picture book, considering that it was about a dog who needed a home.

"Kids, let's give Courtney and Shelby a nice round of applause for that story," Lisa suggested when they were done. "Now, if you have any questions for Courtney, please raise your hand."

"What's her favorite thing to eat?" a little boy in the front row asked.

"She's a pretty typical dog, so she likes any kind of dog treats and bones."

"Does she know how to fetch?" asked a little girl in a pink dress.

"She does," Courtney replied with a smile. "Shelby knows a few simple commands, like fetch, sit, and stay. She's a very smart dog."

"Does she live with you?" This came from a girl in a blue sweater that matched her big eyes. The name Sophie was embroidered across the front of her shirt. "Does she have a home, or is she like the dog in the story?"

Seeing how much the idea affected the poor little girl made tears burn at the backs of Courtney's eyes, even though she was confident that Shelby would have a happy ending to her own story. "Shelby doesn't have a home right now," she said honestly. "She stays at the shelter. That means she's never out in the cold, and she always has food and water. We even have a lady there whose job it is to make sure her fur is brushed and her nails aretrimmed, and she can go to the vet if she needs to. But Shelby is hoping to find a real home someday, in a house with a family who loves her."

"I want to take her home!

"Me, too!"

"I'll feed her!"

The instant offers filled Courtney with love, though she knew that most of these kids had no idea just what it would involve bringing a dog like Shelby home. "I know Shelby is a great dog, and I'm sure all of you would be wonderful with her. It's important to know that having a dog isn't like having stuffed toy. She has to be fed and watered, and someone must be home to take her out to go potty. Pets are a big responsibility. You should talk to your parents about how a dog might fit into your home. I do have a coloring sheet for each of you that has the shelter's information on it, and if your parents want to bring you by, I'd be happy to give you a tour of the shelter."

Lisa took the stack of coloring sheets that they'd already prepared for the evening and began passing them out. "Let's start with the front row, and you can get in line to meet Shelby. Nice and polite, thank you."

Courtney was a little worn out by the time she got through every single child and every single question, especially since a lot of them asked the same ones, but she was also getting charged up about such a wonderful experience. By the time the last child waved goodbye to Shelby and headed off with his mother, Courtney knew they had to do this again. "This was amazing, Lisa. Thank you so much for arranging it."

"Hey, you're the one who did all the hard work," Lisa said with a smile as she straightened the stack of the remaining coloring sheets and set them aside. "And you'll have a lot more hard work ahead of you if any of those kids actually take you up on a free tour of the shelter. They'll be lined up out the door if tonight is any indicator."

"That's all right with me," Courtney said as she gave Shelby a much-deserved treat. "It might be a little bit of work, but my job isn't to just manage the place. I've got to get our message out into the public eye as much as possible. I figure if some of these kids do come in with their parents, then I'll have the chance to talk to them as a family and help them all make the best decision."

"You've got a huge heart, Courtney. I have a hard time imagining you working in some corporate office in the city." Lisa stacked up a few chairs and turned off the lights.

It was true. Courtney had come a long way since she'd been sacked from her job at Miller and Martinez Marketing. At the time, it'd felt like her life was over. She'd made peace with that huge change in her life, though, because it'd led her here. "It's hard even for me to imagine it at this point. I do find myself using a lot of my marketing skills for the shelter, too, whether I'm increasing awareness of homeless pets or coming up with new sales and spa packages for the hotel side. You were an absolute genius when you came up with the idea of story hour, though. I loved it."

The two women wandered over near the circulation desk. "Actually, I was thinking maybe we could expand this into something bigger," Lisa said. "I mentioned a while back that it would be nice to have an event at the library. What if we brought a bunch of the shelter pets in here and had volunteers come in to read to them?"

"Oh!" Courtney could instantly envision it, and her heart was soaring already. "I love it! We could use one of the rooms, like the children's room. Adults and children alike could come spend time with the pets, snuggling with them and talking to them. It would be great therapy for the animals, since they crave a lot more human interaction than we can possibly give them. Some of them might end up with homes, but at the very least it'll be great for the pets and increase awareness of all the homelessness."

"I thought you might like it!" Lisa enthused. "Do you think any cats would be able to participate? Sage is doing amazing on his leash, but I know that's not very common." She'd adopted a dog named Beau as well as the little kitten the dog had fallen in love with. Lisa was spending a lot of time training the cat, but felines weren't quite the same as dogs when it came to meeting the public.

Courtney bit her lip as she thought. "I'm not sure. We might try it with one or two of the calmer ones, or else we can host a different, smaller one in the future where people come to the shelter to read to them."

"No!" came a grumpy voice from further down the circulation desk. "I told you that you owe a fifty-cent late fee. You can't check out any more books until you pay it!"

Looking over, Courtney spotted Glenn sitting at the checkout desk. She'd seen him a few times when she'd come to the library to talk to Lisa, but she hadn't interacted with him very much. He was an older gentleman, probably in his fifties, who favored faded flannel shirts and khakis that looked like they were held together by their last stitch. With his surly expression, he didn't exactly invite conversation.

"I'm sorry," said the young woman who stood in front of him. She didn't even look old enough to drive. "I don't have any change with me, and I need this book for my school project. Is there any way I can bring it back to you later?"

"Sure, you can. And *then* you can check out this book!" He tapped the volume on the desk for emphasis.

Courtney understood that there were rules about these things, but her heart went out to the poor girl. "Can you hold her for me?" she asked as she passed

Shelby's leash to Lisa. She dug around in her purse for some change, walked over, and handed it to Glenn. "That should cover it."

Glenn frowned at the coins in his hand, dumped them in the cash drawer, and poked the payment into the computer with one finger without saying a word.

"Thank you so much!" the girl said, tears shimmering in her eyes. "I've got a huge project due next week. Can I have your name and number so I can pay you back?" She started pulling her cell phone out of her pocket.

Courtney put out a hand to stop her. "Don't worry about it. Just pay it forward when you have the chance."

The girl left, and Courtney thought the drama was over, but Glenn wasn't done with her. "You're the one who brought that mutt in here?" he snarled.

"Shelby is a great dog, and she's very sweet. Would you like to meet her?"

"No, I would not!" he snapped. "You shouldn't have animals in the library. That's not what it's for."

"Oh, it's all right. I got permission from the board, and she's here to help people understand that there are a lot of homeless pets in our community," Courtney tried to explain, although she had a good feeling it wasn't going to go very far.

"I don't care what your message is. Dogs don't belong in the library! I suggest you get it out of here as soon as possible!" He turned away from her toward the computer.

Courtney rejoined Lisa as they headed into the back office to talk some more about their upcoming joint event. She gestured with her head toward the man at the circulation desk. "What's his problem?" she whispered.

Lisa shrugged. "He's been like that ever since I started here, and from what I understand that's how he's been for a long time. I always want to step in and say that someone can pay their late fee another time, especially if it's a kid, but Glenn is technically in the right. The rules are that you're supposed to pay before you get more books."

"I would think he would get fired at any other job for behaving like that," Courtney noted, absently stroking her hand down Shelby's back.

"He's been working here for as long as anyone can remember, and even if you talked to the board about him, they probably wouldn't do anything," Lisa said with a shake of her head. She grabbed a notebook and a pen so they could make some notes. "It was nice of you to pay that girl's fee, though. She's in here a lot, and I get the feeling she's really a great student who studies hard."

"We all make mistakes, and it seems like a little bit of a late fee isn't that bad. I was happy to help," Courtney replied.

The two of them settled in to talk some more about their read-to-a-pet event, and Courtney soon forgot about grumpy Glenn.

CHAPTER THREE

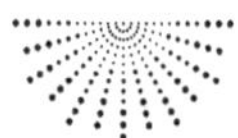

The event was quickly dubbed Books and Barks, and after just a few posts on social media, the idea was taking off quickly. Courtney was always excited when she was able to bring a few animals out into the community, but it was even more thrilling because it was going to be at the library. She'd always loved the library growing up, and now this event would provide that much more information and education to the public.

"Wow," Courtney said as she brought Hansel and Gretel into through the front doors. They were two pug mixes, brother and sister, who had recently come into the shelter. She thought they might be good tagalongs for the signup event. "Lisa, is there some other event going on here today? Like a business development meeting or something?"

Lisa smiled at the crowd that had already assembled in the lobby area in front of the circulation desk and was bleeding over into the stacks. "Nope, this is all for you! I'm sure it doesn't hurt that we said there would be refreshments, but I have to say I'm pretty impressed myself. I see a lot of our regulars, and of course I told every person who came through those doors about it over the last few days."

Courtney spotted several people who had fostered or volunteered at the shelter, including Alex Strickland. A construction worker in his late twenties, he was enthusiastic and energetic. "Hey, Alex! Are you here to sign up?"

He instantly dropped to one knee so he could greet the two dogs, accepting all the kisses they would give him. "Of course! I can't say I'm much into reading, since I'd rather be building something with my hands, but I suppose the dogs wouldn't mind if I read to them from a code manual or an issue of *This Old House*, right?"

"Not at all," Courtney agreed. It really didn't matter what reading material someone picked. "The most important thing is that you enjoy it. I'm glad to see you here."

"I wouldn't miss it for the world, especially considering the cupcakes they put out." Alex rubbed his stomach. "I could make myself sick on those, but I think I'll go get another one."

As Alex walked off, Courtney noticed Glenn sitting at the circulation desk once again. He was glaring at the young construction worker, his frown deepened by the effect of his thick glasses. Courtney guessed Glenn wasn't pleased about the idea of having animals in the library once again for the signup event. "He's really going to be ticked when I bring in all the animals for the official Books and Barks event, and not just the signup day," she said quietly to Lisa.

"I know, but he'll just have to get over it. Is that the donation box? I can set it up over here." Lisa reached out to take the box that Courtney was juggling along with the two dogs.

"Great, thank you. And is there someplace I could plug my phone in? I guess the battery is getting old, and it's giving me fits." She pulled the offending phone and its charger from her purse.

"Sure. I'll take it to the office."

"Courtney! It's so lovely to see you!" Mrs. Throgmorton, one of the biggest supporters of the shelter, came sweeping up. Despite the fact that this was an evening all about the animals, she was wearing a cashmere sweater set and pearls. Courtney noted her expensive perfume as the older woman wrapped her in a polite hug.

"It's good to see you, too. Did you have fun over the holidays?"

Mrs. Throgmorton swished a beringed hand through the air. "Oh, of course, but I'm a little glad it's over with, if I'm honest. All those parties get to be such a drudgery. This year, I'm thinking about taking Sir Glitter and just heading to a remote beach somewhere. It would be far more relaxing."

Courtney was quite familiar with Sir Glitter, a Pomeranian who was a regular at the spa and hotel. "That sounds wonderful. I really appreciate you coming out tonight to show your support."

"Of course! Of course! I wouldn't miss a chance to help out in any little way that I can. I truly do think that the, shall we say, more influential members of the community have a duty to do so. Speaking of, you should really talk to Miles Dorrington about organizing an event or two. He puts in a bit of volunteer work here and there, and he always puts on the best parties in the highest social circles."

"Oh, I'm not so sure that would be a good idea," Courtney said with a shake of her head. "I'm afraid Mr. Dorrington is a little upset with the spa right now. He feels that Dora cut his dog's hair too short, and he's not going to come back. I highly doubt he'd want to help organize a fundraiser."

Mrs. Throgmorton's thin eyebrows lifted up toward her curled hair. "Really? That's interesting, since he's here this evening."

"He is?" Courtney glanced around the room, finally catching sight of him over near the refreshment table. He was a tall, thin man with white hair that matched his shockingly thick mustache. "I'm really surprised."

"Well, his office is just on the other side of the park, and he's at all the library events. Dora is always incredibly careful with her work, so maybe there was some sort of miscommunication," Mrs. Throgmorton theorized.

"I hope so, too. Or at least, something that can be sorted out. I don't like to think of anyone being unhappy with us. Even so, I think I'll give him some space and time. I agree that his influence could be wonderful for the shelter, but I don't want that influence to be a negative one."

"A wise decision," Mrs. Throgmorton agreed. "Not that I expect anything different from you, my dear. Now, here's an idea. There's going to be a big party at the country club this weekend. You should come as my guest, and you can bring Peppa with you."

A wave of heat flushed over Courtney's face at the thought of going to such an affluent place. This was the type of country club that didn't let just anybody in. Anyone new had to be invited by a current member in good standing, and they still had to be approved by a majority of the club. "Are you sure? I wouldn't want to impose, especially on a party."

"Oh, it's not as though it's anything special," Mrs. Throgmorton countered. "They throw parties for any little thing they can come up with. I think this one is supposed to be some sort of winter party, just as an excuse to have something between New Year's and Valentine's Day. Really, I want you to come."

"Well, um, what should I wear?" Courtney knew Mrs. Throgmorton had the best interests of the shelter in mind, and she'd certainly helped pull things together for the shelter before.

"I'll check the invitation and give you a call. Now, if you'll excuse me for just a moment, I see someone I wanted to talk to." Mrs. Throgmorton patted

Courtney on the arm and glided across the room to greet a friend.

Lisa returned just then with a woman in tow. She had long, dark blonde hair that she kept in a braid over her shoulder, and she wore a conservative floral dress. "Courtney, I don't know if you've officially met my other coworker, Nora Gallagher. This is Courtney Cain."

"Nice to meet you," Courtney said, offering her hand.

Nora shook it, her fingers smooth and limp. She had a serious and studious expression on her face, and she didn't even smile. "Yes. You, too," she said before turning and walking away.

"Sorry about that," Lisa said quietly. "She's very much into books, but not so much into people. She could probably answer just about any question a patron could have about a book without having to look it up, and I think she's got our entire catalog memorized."

"We all have our quirks."

The evening went quickly but smoothly, and before Courtney knew it there was a long list of people who'd signed up to read to a pup or two. "I was worried some of the dogs would have to be left out of the program if we didn't have enough volunteers," she noted to Lisa as Hansel stretched out to the end of his leash to snag a cupcake crumb off the floor. "Now, I think I'm more likely to run out of dogs!"

"I knew it would go over well. If the event itself goes the way I think it will, we'll have to do another one when it's warmer outside and we can be in the park."

"Sounds like you're already thinking ahead and looking to expand," Courtney said with a wink as she tucked the signup sheet and a few other papers into a folder. There wasn't anyone left at the library other than Courtney and those who worked there. They would be closing in less than an hour, and Courtney was ready to get home and relax for the evening.

"Now that you mention it, yes," Lisa agreed. "Just the idea of moving it outside to the park made me think of three-legged races, grilled hot dogs, and lemonade. I know it's the middle of winter, but I guess I'm already dreaming about summer."

"That sounds wonderful! So does having some big annual event, something that means we don't have to constantly come up with new ideas. I'll have to work on that." She was already turning over ideas in her head to make it into a day-long event.

"I'll help in any way I can," Lisa reminded her. "I should be able to get in touch with the park district pretty easily. We work with them all the time anyway, since it's right next door."

"I haven't really been to that park much," Courtney admitted, "but it's really pretty with all the trees and benches." She was about to say something else about the park, but whatever it was escaped her mind as she picked up the donation box.

Lisa must have seen the tension in her shoulders. "What's wrong?"

Wanting to make sure, Courtney picked up the box. It was a simple plastic container with a slot cut in the lid and information about the shelter pasted onto the front, but it didn't make the typical jangle of coins and money inside when she moved it around. She lifted the lid to see that it was completely empty. "This isn't right. I know I saw quite a few people put cash in here."

"Did you have it locked?" Lisa asked.

Courtney closed her eyes and hefted a deep sigh. "No. We never have because the hasp is broken. It's the same box the shelter has been using for years. I talked to Ms. O'Donnell about getting a different one, but she said she didn't want to spend the money on a new one. We've never had this problem before."

"And there's no chance you could've emptied it out partway through the night and tucked the money into a safe spot?" Lisa asked.

Courtney put her head in her hand. "No, I'm afraid not. Somebody stole it."

"That's just crazy."

"I know, but it's the only thing that makes sense right now. Do you mind if I step into your office to get my phone off the charger? I think we need to call the police."

"It's okay. I've got it." Lisa took her own cell out of her pocket and dialed.

CHAPTER FOUR

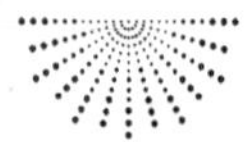

Courtney jumped when a heavy knock sounded on the locked library doors, a precaution they'd taken just to make themselves feel better. Detective Fletcher, looked tired and bored as always, stood just outside under the yellow light of the outdoor lamp. Lisa quickly ran to let him in.

"Okay, let's hear it," he said, his monotone echoing through the quiet library. "You say some money was stolen?"

"Yes. We were doing a signup for an event we're having here for the shelter, and I'd brought a donation box for anyone who wanted to drop in a little money. I know they did, so there should be something in there, but when we went to clean up it was almost completely empty." Courtney opened the box to show him.

Detective Fletcher peered inside and nodded. "I see. And are there any security cameras in here? That could clear things up pretty quickly, you know."

Lisa's cheeks were pink. "I'm afraid not. The library board has discussed it, but we don't have the funding. Most of the time, there's not much need for putting security cameras up for some books and a few late fees."

Glenn grumbled something unintelligible from his seat behind the circulation desk.

"Mmm, that's too bad. Can you tell me a little bit about the night? Was anyone alone with the donation box?"

"I really don't know," Courtney admitted. She pressed her fingers to her forehead as she tried to put it all together. "I had the box when I came in. Lisa put it on the table over there for me, the one near the circulation desk. I don't think I paid much attention to it the rest of the night, until it was time to go, anyway."

"This table here?" Detective Fletcher walked over to the small, circular table just to the left of the circulation desk. It was where the library often put out coloring pages for children or handouts about upcoming events. He tapped the laminated surface. "Right out in front of everything, and yet also over here where the lights are just a little darker. Shorter than the circulation desk, so probably not the best choice."

"No, I suppose not," Lisa said quietly.

"Don't think of this as being your fault, not at all," Courtney advised. "I'm the one who didn't have a lock on it. Even with that, I should've been watching more carefully."

"Is there anyone who might have a reason to take the money?" Fletcher asked, giving Courtney a knowing look. "As you know, a motive can be helpful."

Courtney knew exactly why he looked at her like that. Courtney had been of assistance on several cases since she'd come to Curly Bay. She certainly didn't think of herself as a detective, but when things were constantly happening around her, she often found the urge to get to the bottom of them. Courtney tapped her fingers against her chin. "I've been thinking about that while we waited for you to arrive. The thing is, most of the people here were pretty affluent, or at least well enough off that I can't imagine them having any reason for taking a handful of cash. Mrs. Throgmorton was here to show her support, and even Miles Dorrington. I saw Alex Strickland, and even though he works in construction I get the idea that he stays pretty steadily employed throughout the year. I really don't know."

"I'll tell you who did it." Nora Gallagher marched up, her fists curled at her sides. She still had that odd, neutral expression, but Courtney thought she detected some anger simmering underneath it. When Courtney had last seen her, she'd been making the most use of her time by putting some books back in the stacks, but apparently she'd felt strongly enough about this to face the other humans in the room. "It was Glenn Hughes. I have no doubt."

"Did you see him take it?" Detective Fletcher was never one to overreact, and sometimes Courtney felt that he didn't react enough at all. That sense of calm was nice and reliable, though.

Nora gave the slightest shake of her head. "I didn't see him, but I don't need to. He was sitting at the circulation desk the whole night, so he's the only one who had any chance of seeing someone take the money. In fact, I think he was alone with the donation box at one point in the evening while the dogs were putting on a little show."

"A show?" Detective Fletcher asked, raising one steely gray eyebrow.

Courtney shook her head. "They were just playing together. They get kind of loud with all their little grunts and growls, and they were attracting a lot of attention." She bent down to pat Hansel and Gretel, who were now sitting patiently at her feet.

"I see. But you didn't actually see him take the money?" the detective pressed.

"Well, no," Nora admitted, although she looked annoyed at being called out on such a small detail. "But I know he's been having some sort of money problems. If there's anyone here who had a reason to do it, it's him. You should arrest him right now."

Detective Fletcher pulled in a deep breath. "Miss, you have to understand that I can't go making accusations or arrests simply because you *think* something happened. That's not how these things work."

"I see how it is. Just another law enforcer, paid by our tax dollars, who refuses to deliver justice. I'll be making a note of this, Detective Fletcher, and if I were you I would expect to hear from your superiors." Nora frowned.

"You go right ahead." Fletcher was clearly not affected by her claims.

"I know Glenn did it, and it's an atrocity that you won't listen to me!"

"What?" Glenn had apparently stepped into the other room during all this, because as he came back in now and caught the last part of the conversation, he came marching up. "Are you accusing me of stealing the money?"

Nora lifted her shoulders in a challenge. "Why shouldn't I? You dress like you went dumpster diving behind a thrift store, and I've seen you sweating every time you balance your checkbook at your desk. You've got a money problem, and I don't need to know the details to understand that money —or rather a lack thereof—is usually a bigger motivator than anything else when someone commits a crime."

Glenn was always rather surly looking, but the grumpy look on his face turned into one of pure rage. "How dare you accuse me? I balance my cash drawer down to the last cent every night. I guard this library from all the little ruffians who come in here as though my life depends on it. I might not care for this woman and all her dogs, but I wouldn't steal from them!"

"It's all right, Mr. Hughes," Detective Fletcher said calmly. "Nobody is accusing you of anything. We're just trying to hash out all the facts that we can."

"Yeah, right! You're all standing there looking at me like I'm some sort of criminal! I don't have to take this!" He stormed over behind the circulation desk, grabbed his coat, and left.

Courtney had a feeling he would've slammed the door behind him if it didn't have automatic closers that prevented him from doing so. "I'm sorry about that, Detective Fletcher. I'm afraid we're all a little tired and spooked, and we're not much help."

"That's all right," he assured her. "Let me just make a copy of your signup sheet to get a start on who might've been here tonight. I'll call you soon."

When he'd left, Nora had her jacket and her handbag at the ready. "I'm heading home as well. Are you locking up?"

"Yeah, go on home. I've got this." Lisa waited until she was gone before turning to Courtney. "Can you believe her? Accusing Glenn like that? She didn't even bother to make sure she did it privately!"

"The two of them don't have some sort of feud going on, do they?" Courtney asked, having wondered about Nora's behavior herself. "I mean, that was pretty bold and pretty rude, especially since there isn't any actual evidence."

"Neither one of them is very friendly, so it's hard to say," she replied with a sigh. "What do you think? Could we recreate everything that happened here tonight and figure out who did this?"

Courtney checked her watch. "It's getting pretty late. I've still got to get Hansel and Gretel back to the shelter and get home to Peppa. Even if that was a factor, I think there were just too many people here to really figure it out."

Lisa nodded. "Give me a second to lock up and I'll walk with you. You're on the other side of the park, right?"

"Yep." There were only a few parking spots right by the library, and most folks parked at the community lot on the other side of the park.

"I thought so. I've heard it's really not the safest place to walk through by yourself at night." Lisa went around behind the circulation desk to turn off the computer.

"Really? I hadn't heard anything about that." Not that she necessarily had any reason to, but it was still a bit discomforting to know.

Lisa shrugged. "Well, I haven't heard anything specific. It's just sort of a rumor, and a feeling. I did go through there one night alone when I closed up. I'm not the sort of girl who's afraid of the dark, but I felt like someone was watching me. During the day, everyone who has offices or is doing business in this part of town cuts through it."

Courtney chewed her lip. "Great. That's just what we need after the kind of evening we've had."

"We'll be all right as long as we're together."

The two women stepped outside, and Lisa locked the door behind them. She grabbed the handle and shook it just to make sure it was secure before they headed for the path that cut through the park.

"If you need any help figuring out who stole that money, just let me know," Lisa said as she pulled her scarf closer around her neck against the chilly night. "I just hope that we get it figured out before the weather gets bad. If we get all the ice and snow they're talking about, then it won't be good weather for doing anything."

"Why is everyone so convinced we're going to have bad weather?" Courtney asked. Hansel and Gretel jogged along happily through the park, their tongues hanging out the sides of their mouths in glee. "Jessi and Dora were talking about it at work, too."

"This year's almanac says it's going to be bad," Lisa replied. "Beyond that, I'm not sure."

"Do we know when this terrible storm is supposed to hit?" Courtney asked. "I've been told I should be prepared, and I haven't even made it to the grocery store yet."

Lisa tipped her head back to look at the dark, cloudy sky above them. "I don't have a clue."

"Oh, look at that." Courtney slowed as they passed one of the numerous benches in the park. They were near the very center of the space, farthest from any parking lots or buildings. A red checkered blanket, worn and dirty around the edges, was draped over the back of it. A bundle of equally ratty clothing was folded neatly in a small stack on the seat of the bench. "Someone must be sleeping here."

Lisa frowned. "Odd. I've never noticed any homeless people in Curly Bay before."

"Me, neither. It was pretty common in the city, but I guess I haven't thought about it at all since I've moved here. Are there any shelters in town?" Her heart went out to whoever was trying to make it out here, where the only shelter offered was from the bare trees that rattled overhead. She did everything in her power to help the cats, dogs, and sometimes other animals of Curly Bay stay safe and warm. She hoped that someone was doing the same for humans, too.

"I don't know of one," Lisa admitted.

Squinting into the darkness under the trees, Courtney thought she saw a knapsack sitting at the base of one of them. "I'll call Detective Fletcher when I get the dogs settled in. Maybe he can do something to help."

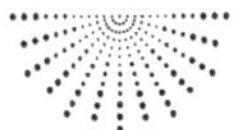

Courtney sat at her desk with a big legal pad. She'd split it down the middle to create two columns for Books and Barks. One was for things she needed to do, and the other was for supplies she would need to bring. "Do you think Peggy would do well at the library?" she asked as Jessi came through the office from the shelter side. "She's come a long way since we first got her in here."

Jessi paused and leaned against her desk. "Yeah, probably. I think we just need a contingency plan to be able to bring any dog who isn't doing well back to the shelter."

Tapping her pen on her paper, Courtney nodded. "That could be a little bit of a problem. Whoever transports them would need to be one of us, since the building will be locked. I can't just leave all those dogs at the library without one of us, either. Are you going to be able to come?"

"I wouldn't miss it for the world," Jessi said with a nod as she took her lunch out of her desk and sat down. "I'm sorry I didn't say that before. I guess I just assumed I would be going, no matter what."

"I don't like to assume anything," Courtney replied, adding Peggy's name to the list of dogs who would be joining the program. "I get so excited about these events when I'm just starting to get the ideas for them, but it's a lot more stressful to actually plan them out. I worry about what might go wrong."

"And in this case, that could be the weather," Jessi pointed out as she took a wrapped sandwich from her lunch bag. "Do we have a backup date in case we get iced or snowed out?"

"No," Courtney admitted. "I keep forgetting that everyone around here is currently obsessed with winter weather. I'll text Lisa and see if there's another night that might work just in case. Or not." Her phone was dead once again, and she put it on the charger.

"I'm telling you, you really need to get that taken care of," Jessi said. "If you're concerned about having time to do it during the workday, then don't worry about us. We can hold down the fort."

"It's not that. I've just been busy, and—"

"Courtney!"

Courtney automatically jumped up from her desk and rushed out to the lobby where she'd heard the voice coming from. She'd heard the desperation in that shout, and her blood was pumping through her body as she came out of the office to see Lisa rushing in through the lobby. "What is it? What's wrong?"

Lisa's eyes were wide, and there were small beads of sweat around the edges of her hair despite the chilly day. "I had to tell you as soon as I found out. I tried to call you on your cell, but I couldn't get through. I wasn't even sure I *wanted* to say it over the phone, so I thought I'd come over here. They've had to close down the library for the day, anyway."

Courtney reached across the counter and grabbed Lisa's arm. "Calm down. Whatever it is, it's all going to be okay. Now slow down and tell me what happened." She let go of her friend long enough to come through the gate that separated the lobby from the rest of the building. She guided Lisa to a chair.

Whatever had happened had affected the librarian deeply. Lisa was a pretty calm person, and Courtney couldn't remember ever seeing her like this. She currently looked like she was going to pass out, and Courtney had to wonder how Lisa had been able to get to the shelter safely. "When I got to work to open up the building for the day, I could see the lights of emergency vehicles over by the park. One of the officers came into the library to talk to me. Oh, Courtney, they found Glenn! He's dead!"

"What?" Courtney could hardly believe her ears. "Do they have any idea what happened?"

"If they do, they haven't told me. I didn't see Detective Fletcher there, or I would've asked him. They asked me all sorts of questions about him, though, and I think they at least suspect foul play." Her arm was shaking under Courtney's hand.

"That's strange. Glenn left before we did. If something happened to him when he was going through the park on his way home, then wouldn't we have seen it?" Courtney tried to wrap her brain around this one.

"I guess so. I mean, that makes sense. I don't know exactly where in the park they found him, though. I didn't ask, and I'm not sure I want to know." Lisa ran a hand through her hair and took a deep breath. "I'm sorry. I shouldn't have freaked out like that. I was just expecting a typical winter day at the library, with Glenn grumbling about kids tracking in water and mud. He was kind of terrible, but I think I'm still going to miss him."

"That's completely understandable," Courtney soothed. She pulled in a breath to speak but paused, realizing this probably wasn't the right time.

"Go ahead," Lisa said with a little laugh. "You're already thinking about who could've done this, right?"

"Well, you know me," Courtney said. "And this kind of builds off all our ideas about the stolen donation money, doesn't it? First, we've got Nora. She obviously has a problem with Glenn, or else she wouldn't have accused him so openly."

Lisa nodded. "She's definitely got a problem with him, but I think it's just that she doesn't like working with him. That, and they're both incredibly bad-tempered. I'm not sure she's got a reason to actually murder him, though."

"Maybe not," Courtney admitted. "I also saw the way Glenn was glaring at Alex Strickland. Do you remember him?"

"The construction guy, right?" Some of the color was starting to return to Lisa's cheeks, and she wasn't shaking so badly anymore. Maybe the distraction of solving the case was helping.

Courtney knew it always helped her, anyway. It made her feel as though she was doing something to help, and that was important to her. "Right. He volunteers here all the time, and he's never been anything short of polite. I guess that's why I thought it was so odd that Glenn seemed so upset with him. I don't suppose he owes the library a dollar or two, does he?" She said it half in jest, but Glenn had been a stickler for those late fees.

"Not that I can think of off the top of my head, but it's possible. I can check the computer at the library tomorrow. Like I said, we're closed for the day, considering what's happened."

"Right. I have a hard time believing two grown men would get into some sort of deadly battle over a few cents' worth of late fees, but it's still worth looking into. Is there anybody else who might've had a problem with Glenn?" Courtney speculated.

Lisa let out a little laugh. "Probably everybody in Curly Bay. I mean, you saw the way he treated that girl who owed fifty cents. He acted like she was lower than scum, and that's kind of how he is to everybody."

"Manners are important, but they're not worth killing over," Courtney noted. She closed her eyes and thought about the previous night, hoping some vital detail would suddenly resurface. Unfortunately, it was just as much of a blur for her now as it'd been when she'd tried to figure out who might've stolen the money. She was just about to suggest getting the signup sheet when she remembered something. "What about the person sleeping in the park?"

"The homeless person? I guess it's possible. Too bad we don't know who that is." Lisa shook her head. "Even so, I don't like the idea of accusing someone of such a horrible act simply because they're homeless."

"No, and I don't either," Courtney agreed quickly. "But I didn't even necessarily mean to bring them up as a suspect. To me, that could be a witness."

"Oh, right. If they were in the park when something happened to Glenn, they might have some valuable information."

Courtney leaned forward and braced her elbows on her knees as she thought. The world was such a big place, but it was in the small town of Curly Bay where she'd been able to see just how interconnected everything was. Even knowing that didn't make it easy to figure out what was happening around them, though. "My question is if someone in that position would be willing to talk to the police. I saw plenty of officers in the city who were willing to help those in need, whether that was giving them a ride to a shelter or helping them getting enrolled in various programs. In general, though, there were plenty of vagrants who did their best to hide from any authorities."

"Had you talked to Detective Fletcher about this person last night?" Lisa asked. She looked even better now, almost as though they hadn't been sitting there in the lobby talking about murder.

"I was able to send him a text, and he said he'd look into it, but I imagine he's even busier than he already was now that they have a body on their hands. I'll bug him about it again, though. I'm sure he's already thought about it, considering both the murderer and the homeless person were in the park." Courtney sat back and patted her knees. "I guess you really weren't kidding about that park being unsafe at night."

Lisa stood up and rubbed her hands over her face. "I know. And he used to go through there by himself all the time to go home. He never would wait for any of us. I guess I'd better let you get back to your day."

"As much as I can. I'll have this on my mind the entire time," Courtney replied truthfully, even though she did have things she needed to do. "Do you need a ride home or anything?"

"No, I think I'll be fine. Beau and Sage will be happy to have me home for the day. I think I'll just turn on some old movies and curl up with a hot mug of tea."

"Sounds like a good plan. I'll call you later." Courtney watched her leave the parking lot, happy to see that she did look a lot steadier than she'd been when she'd first arrived. Still, she knew she wouldn't be able to stop thinking about what happened to Glenn. He really had been a lead suspect in the stolen money, but what did it mean for the case now that he was dead?

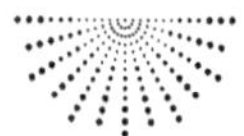

CHAPTER SIX

Courtney looked in her pantry and jotted some notes down. She was usually pretty good about keeping plenty of groceries on hand, but either the holidays or just her work at the shelter had been keeping her far too busy. There were more empty spaces on the shelves than there were full ones. She added green beans and potatoes to her list as Peppa came trotting in the kitchen to see what she was doing.

"Hey, sweetness," Courtney cooed as she set down her list to rub the dog's ears. "Anything you want from the store?"

Thought it was probably only because it was her dinner time, Peppa headed over to the big bin where Courtney kept the dog kibble and wagged her tail.

Courtney laughed. "Don't worry, sweetheart. I already have that on the list, and a few treats as well."

Peppa followed her to the front door when she saw Courtney grab her keys and put on her coat.

"I'm sorry. They don't allow dogs in the grocery store, no matter how wonderful they are. I know it's hard on you when you do get to go so many places with me, but you'll have to stay here and guard the fort for me, okay?" Courtney tossed her a treat, gave her one last pat, and headed outside.

A few flakes of snow were spiraling down from the dark sky. They dashed across Courtney's windshield and whisked off into the night as she drove through town, accumulating on the edges of yards and in the gutters. It was still a light snow, though, and it wasn't enough of one to make her worry.

What did make her worry a little more was the sheer number of cars at the store. The parking lot was far too full for a midweek evening. Shoppers hustled back and forth as they loaded their carts, and Courtney noted the looks of desperation on their faces. Was she really the only one who was just here to make a regular shopping trip? It looked like everyone else in Curly Bay was stocking up for the apocalypse. That was all right. She would just be in and out for a few staples, and then she'd be done.

But what she found in the store wasn't quite so simple. The bread aisle was almost completely wiped out, leaving just a few lonely packages of hot dog buns. Courtney only went through a small amount of milk each week, since she lived alone, but even the smallest containers were already gone. The same thing had happened all over the store. Everyone had come in and snapped up all the basics. Her cart was hardly full at all by the time she headed over to the pet food section.

Courtney always saved this part of her shopping trip for last. Bags of dog food were heavy, after all, and she didn't want to push fifty pounds of kibble all over the store. As she threaded her way through the crowd, however, she began to worry that she would find empty shelves just as she had everywhere else.

As she came around the corner, her shoulders sagged in relief when she saw two bags of the food Peppa liked still on the shelf. She only took one, knowing someone else would be just as happy to find the food as she was. After grabbing a bag of treats and, just for fun, a special squeaky toy, Courtney began making her way to the checkout.

Unfortunately, this part of the store was just as frustrating. Only a few of the checkout lanes were open, and the lines reached all the way back across the main walkway and into the aisle. With a sigh, Courtney joined one of the queues. She waited behind an older woman who kept looking at her wallet.

As she did, she couldn't help but think about whoever had been sleeping in the park. All these people in the store were busy preparing for the bad weather they believed was coming. What about someone who had no home to hunker down in? Who had no way of making sure they were stocked up on food or firewood? The more she thought about it, the more it bothered her. Since the line was moving slowly anyway, Courtney decided to give Detective Fletcher a call.

"I hope you have something good for me," he said by way of answering. "I'm up to my eyeballs in paperwork right now, not even including your missing money or Glenn Hughes. Whom, I'm assuming, you already know about."

Leave it to Detective Fletcher to be matter-of-fact. "I do. That's sort of why I'm calling you. I was actually wondering if there's anything I can do to help whoever it is that's staying in the park. Everyone says the weather is going to get terrible, and that person need some sort of shelter."

Fletcher sighed. "First, I'm going to tell you not to do something crazy like inviting a stranger to stay with you just because you feel sorry for them. Stray people aren't the same as stray dogs, and I know what a tendency you have for getting yourself into trouble."

Courtney rolled her eyes, even though she knew the detective's advice was sound. Though she hadn't been planning to do any such thing, she might've if the right situation came up. "I'm just concerned. I thought maybe there was someone I could call, or maybe items I could donate. I don't know."

"Well, I can tell you that the entire police department was all over that park this morning. We didn't find any evidence that someone was staying there, so I don't think you have anything to worry about."

Courtney frowned as her eyes wandered over a nearby candy bar display. She clearly remembered the red checkered blanket and the pile of clothes on the bench. It was hard to imagine that they'd simply disappeared. "Nothing?"

"Not a thing. If someone had been there, then they've moved on."

"But where would they go? Is there a shelter or something?" Worry stabbed through her heart as she imagined what it must be like for anyone who didn't have a place to stay. She'd been fortunate enough not to have to worry about that in her lifetime, but she knew others hadn't.

"No, I can't say that there is. We do what we can with a few social programs here in Curly Bay, but homelessness hasn't been a big issue. My guess is it's because people don't really come to a little, out-of-the-way place like this unless they have a good reason, like family. It's not exactly a destination, you know?"

"No, I suppose not." The line moved forward a little further. Courtney noticed the woman in front of her was now frantically counting her cash and then looking in her cart.

"Look, if it makes you feel any better, I can drive by the park tonight and do a quick check. I have a few other stops to make anyway, and it won't hurt. I doubt anyone would want to stay there now, though, with all that crime scene tape up between the trees," Fletcher grumbled.

"I'd really appreciate that," Courtney said hopefully. "But what will you do with someone if you find them? They won't get arrested, will they?"

"No, nothing like that. I can arrange for them to spend the night at the station, completely free to go whenever they want to. Now, as to whether a vagrant would trust me enough to do that is another matter, but I can try."

"Thank you so much," Courtney enthused, genuinely grateful that Detective Fletcher was such a good person. He might grumble a bit and act as though he didn't really want to do his job, but she'd seen the spark in his eye when things went right. She knew that he was looking out for the best interests of everyone in Curly Bay.

"You're very welcome. And now that I've done you this favor, perhaps you can do one for me, if you have any pertinent information on the Glenn Hughes case. I doubt you've been keeping your nose clean."

Courtney had to smile at that one. Detective Fletcher knew her well, and now that they'd worked together several times, he'd come to accept that she was going to get involved whether he liked it or not.

He still liked to lecture her on safety, but she didn't mind. That was just another way she knew he cared. "As a matter of fact, I plan to stick it in some research tomorrow. I don't know anything yet, but I'll call you as soon as I do."

"I have no doubt of that. In the meantime, be safe, Miss Cain."

"Will do."

As she pocketed her cell, Courtney realized she was next in line. The woman in front of her was putting her items on the belt, which included a small bag of potatoes, a box of pasta, a jar of tomato sauce, and a block of cheese. She'd apparently not had any better luck than Courtney in finding milk or bread, but she did have a small, light-up keyboard toy that went next. This was followed by a bag of cat food so small it made Courtney want to laugh. She was used to buying in bulk for all the kitties at the shelter, and she'd nearly forgotten that they even made bags that small.

"That's be fifty-six eighty-four," the young cashier said when everything was bagged up.

"Oh, my. Oh, dear. Let me see what I can do here." She anxiously counted her money once again. "I don't quite have that much. Let's put the toy back. It was for my granddaughter, but she has plenty to play with already."

The cashier pulled it out of the bad and adjusted the total. "Forty-five twenty-two."

The woman frowned. "I'm so sorry. I'll have to think about this. I only have forty. I try to keep a running total in my head while I'm shopping, but this poor old brain doesn't work like it used to." She let out a nervous laugh as she glanced in the grocery bags. "Maybe the potatoes."

"The cat food would take care of it," the cashier offered.

"Yes, but my Rosalyn only has a bowlful left, and I don't want her to be hungry when the storm hits."

Courtney couldn't watch any more. "I'll pay the difference," she offered.

The old woman's gaze lifted to her with hope, but she shook her head. "I can't let you do that. I don't have any way of paying you back until next month."

"You don't need to." Courtney took out the emergency cash she kept in the back of her wallet and handed it to the cashier. "Put the toy back on the bill, too."

"God bless you," the woman said as the cashier put her bags in her cart. "I can't thank you enough."

"It's not a problem." Courtney watched her go, feeling almost guilty for being able to afford what she'd bought. She was always good at budgeting, and she didn't like to be frivolous with money, but she doubted that the poor woman was in this situation because she'd blown all her grocery money on something senseless.

"We see a lot of that, you know," the cashier noted as he began to ring up Courtney's items.

"People paying for others' groceries?" she asked hopefully.

"Senior citizens who can't buy their food," he replied, his face somber. He was young, probably no older than twenty, but it was clear that he was very aware of the way others were suffering. "They're living off their social security, but the cost of food just keeps going up. At least, that's what my mom tells me. I only just moved out on my own, so I've got no comparison."

"It's a shame," Courtney agreed. At least she'd been able to help one person, but who would help the next? Her mind was heavy as she headed out into the parking lot a few minutes later to find that a thin film of snow had accumulated on her car while she'd been in the store. It was just the light, fluffy stuff that swept off easily and was no cause for concern.

CHAPTER SEVEN

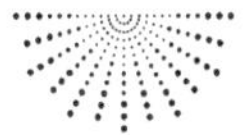

It felt very strange to be heading back into the library the next day. The last time she'd been there, the donation money had been stolen. More recently, she'd received the news about Glenn. For the first time in her life, the library was the last place Courtney wanted to be.

Of course, it was also the best source of information in all of Curly Bay, and she had someone who knew how to make the most of that information. Lisa was sitting at her place behind the circulation desk, but she looked up with a small smile when she saw Courtney. "Did you have plenty of coffee this morning? Because I have big plans for us."

"Then it's a good thing I have the day off." Courtney had plenty of things she ought to be doing with her day off work, but Glenn Hughes had become the top priority on her list. It truly bothered her that something happened to the man, even if he was a grump. "And yes, I've had plenty of coffee."

"Good. Nora, if you've got the desk for a bit, I'm going to help Courtney look up some information." Lisa turned to her coworker as she stood.

Nora glared up at Courtney and then back at Lisa. "Don't be too long. I don't want to be late for my break today."

"Don't worry. I won't get lost in the archives." Lisa locked her computer and led the way down a short hall and to a room separate from the rest of the library.

"I don't want my research to create a problem for you," Courtney said when they were alone. "You can just show me where you keep everything, and I'll take it from there."

Lisa made a face. "Don't worry about Nora. She's always like that, even though nobody has ever stopped her from taking her breaks. I think maybe she just doesn't trust people. Besides, I went into library science because I love research. I think there's something exciting about digging up information and finding one thing that leads to another. I want to be in on this, too, especially since we're talking about Glenn."

"Good, because you probably know how to do it all a lot faster than I do. This isn't going to be like just pulling things up on the internet, although that can be a rabbit hole in itself." She glanced around at the all the filing cabinets that filled the room, wondering if they'd actually be able to find anything.

"Well, we're going to start with the internet. Come here." A table in the center of the room held two PCs on one side and two microfiche machines on the other. Lisa signed in to one of the PCs and pulled up a website. "Our county puts all their court data on a public file. You can't see every tiny detail, but you can see when someone has been arrested or on trial."

"Wouldn't we already know if something like that had happened to Glenn?" Courtney asked as she pulled up a chair.

"Sure, if it was something like that, but it's at least a good place to start. Let's see what we can see under Glenn's name." She rattled it out on the keyboard and hit enter. "Okay. Looks like he filed bankruptcy about a year ago. That's a start."

"Okay, so Nora was right about Glenn having money issues. Not that it was hard to figure out, considering the state of his clothes. I still don't think that means he necessarily stole the money." It cast some doubt in Courtney's mind, but her instincts were telling her that it wasn't him.

"I agree. Let's see what this one is." There was another listing underneath the bankruptcy. When Lisa clicked on it, they both scanned through the details. Lisa was obviously more used to looking at such things, though, because she had it sorted out quickly. "This is interesting. It's a dispute between Glenn and Alex Strickland that went all the way to court. Looks like they were fighting over a piece of property. Whatever the problem was, Alex won."

"I wish we had more details on this," Courtney lamented. It looked like something that could really be relevant, but only if she knew what'd actually happened.

"We can find them!" Lisa quickly opened a new tab and typed in the address for a different site. "Our county also has an online plat map. Not all of them do, so we're kind of lucky. This will at least let me find out if my hunch is correct."

Courtney watched as Lisa checked the address listed for Glenn on the first tab before finding it on the plat map. "You can find out who owns a specific piece of land by hovering over it. Like this." She hovered over the spot that matched Glenn's address. "That's interesting."

"That's not his name." Courtney squinted at the screen. "That looks like a bank, but it's not one that I've heard of before."

"My guess is that he gave the house back in the bankruptcy. I don't think he ever changed his address with us." Lisa hovered over the other address listed on the court documentation. "Alex Strickland is his neighbor, though. Or he was, until recently. I was just coming to the plat map to see if they lived near each other, and I was right, but I wasn't quite expecting this."

"Where do we go from here?" Courtney asked. Nothing was definitive, but she was glad they were at least finding something. They were piecing together Glenn's life, and she wanted to know more.

Lisa was already on it. "The court files have only been added over the last few years, but we can search for his name in the newspapers and older court records and see if we can come up with anything else."

Courtney was incredibly grateful for Lisa. "You really do know your stuff, don't you?"

"Like I said, I was always into this stuff. I was the geeky kid who actually enjoyed doing the research for essays and papers. It's just so interesting, even when we're just talking about the minutiae of someone's daily life. Okay, here we go. We've got some newspaper articles that mention his name. I'll pull up the microfiche." She quickly rifled through several file drawers and moved around to the machines on the other side of the table.

Courtney's eyes reeled as Lisa skimmed through the microfiche. "Wow. This looks old."

"It is. It was the first entry, and it's probably not relevant, but I figured it was a place to start. This is from when Glenn was a kid." She pulled up an article that detailed a young boy by the name of Glenn Hughes who had been attacked by a dog.

"It says he was walking home from school when the dog escaped its yard, bowled him over, and bit him several times," Courtney read before studying the photo of a very young Glenn. He wasn't any happier in this picture than Courtney had ever seen him in real life. "No wonder he was so upset about having dogs in the library. He was probably scared."

"Let's see what the next one has to offer." Lisa changed out the film and located a small blurb in the public records. "This is much newer. This was only a few years before everything went online."

"Divorce." Just as in the online records, it was a simple statement of facts. They could see that Glenn and his wife had divorced, but there was nothing to show all the details. "That could've led to the bankruptcy. I've seen it happen before. If Glenn was the one who was left with the house or other bills, and if he had to pay any alimony or child support, he might've been having a really hard time recovering from divorce."

"So where does this leave us so far?" Lisa asked.

Courtney straightened, blinking her eyes as she looked at reality again instead of a screen. "I'm not sure. I would say it moves Alex Strickland a little more to the forefront of the list of murder suspects, since we know for sure that the two of them had a dispute, but Alex won the case. Whatever they were fighting over isn't relevant, especially since Glenn doesn't own that house anymore."

"What about the ex-wife?" Lisa speculated. "We don't know which one of them filed for divorce or what the reasons were. I've read plenty of murder mysteries to know that passion can be quite the motivator."

"A possibility, but it just doesn't feel right." Courtney didn't know how to explain it, but she just had a feeling they were looking in the wrong direction. She was glad to know more about Glenn, because it felt like a little bit of a memorial to him. But it wasn't getting them any closer to his killer. "You know what bothers me?"

"What's that?" Lisa replaced the microfiche documents carefully.

"I'm not sure right now if we're looking for Glenn's murderer or for the person who stole the donation money." Courtney had been thinking about this quite a bit ever since she'd heard of his death. "I mean, do we think the stolen money has anything to do with the murder? Or is it purely coincidental?"

Lisa leaned against a filing cabinet. "I would think that if they found the money on Glenn, Detective Fletcher would've told you about it."

"Providing that he did steal it, who's to say that his killer wouldn't have stolen the money? What if someone knew he had the extra cash and killed him for it?" She pulled in a deep breath and looked up at the ceiling. "I just wish I could figure it all out."

"Are you ladies done with your little gossip session?" an aggravated voice said from the doorway. "It's only ten minutes until my break, you know."

"I'm fully aware of that, Nora," Lisa said calmly. "We're just finishing up."

Nora gave her a doubtful look before slowly turning and heading back down the hall.

Courtney frowned. "Do you think she would know anything about Glenn's death? I mean, did the two of them talk or spend any time together?"

"Like I said before, you're talking about the two least friendly people on the face of the planet," Lisa replied. "If Glenn had any secrets to share, then I doubt he told her. You could ask her if you wanted."

"I'll think about it. I'm not sure it's worth the verbal torture she'll no doubt put me through." Courtney brushed her dark, straight hair behind her ear and pulled in a deep breath. "I'll keep my distance for the moment. Thanks for your help today."

"Any time. I enjoyed it. Oh, did you ever get your phone fixed? I meant to tell you I sent you a text earlier today, but it didn't seem to go through."

Courtney's shoulders slumped. "Do you have any idea how much spare time I'm finding these days now that I'm not constantly looking at my phone?"

"Get it fixed so you can call me late at night when you finally break the case," Lisa advised. "You can't keep me waiting in suspense until you get a landline!"

Courtney laughed as she left the library, but the smile faded from her face as she glanced at the seat at the circulation desk where Glenn used to sit. Whether he'd stolen the money or not, she had a murder to solve.

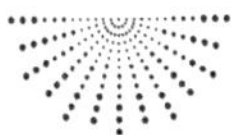

CHAPTER EIGHT

Courtney smoothed down the dark purple dress she'd put on for the evening. The air had taken a sudden chill this evening, and it went straight through the fabric. The small shrug she'd topped the dress with wasn't enough to stop it, and Courtney was grateful that the country club had plenty of good parking.

"Come on, Peppa," she said as she locked her car. "I know you've been to all sorts of events around Curly Bay, and you've met all sorts of people, but we have to be on our absolute best behavior while we're here. No begging or drooling, okay?"

Peppa, who wore a pink sweater and didn't seem to mind the cold at all as long as she was on an adventure, happily trotted along at her side.

Heading quickly up the sweeping steps that fronted the huge clubhouse, Courtney tugged open one of the huge double doors and found herself inside a foyer. To the left was a coat check, and through another set of double doors in front of her she could see that the party had already started.

A gentleman in a suit stepped out from behind a small podium and frowned at her. "Ma'am, dogs aren't allowed in the clubhouse."

Courtney's face burned with heat despite the chill that had blown in through the door behind her. She was always very aware of any establishment's rules when it came to animals, and it was rare that she encountered something like this. "I understand, but Peppa here is a special guest of Mrs. Throgmorton."

"Do you have an invitation?" the man asked, lifting his chin slightly so that he looked down his nose at her.

"I'm afraid not." Mrs. Throgmorton hadn't said anything about an invitation, had she? "Perhaps you could check with Mrs. Throgmorton. She might be here already."

The man pressed his lips together and stepped back behind his podium to scan a list just as Mrs. Throgmorton herself came through the doors from the main area of the clubhouse. "James! I hope you weren't giving my guests a hard time! Come right on in, Courtney. Let's get you out of the cold. You look chilled!"

James glared at her as she passed through the double doors into a vast common area. The ceiling was lined with solid wood timbers, and faux lanterns dangled down between them. Circular tables draped in white were interspersed with comfortable looking seating areas of leather and thick, luxurious décor fabrics. Mrs. Throgmorton led her straight to a fireplace with an opening almost as tall as she was, which was roaring with flames. A drink appeared seemingly out of nowhere, and Mrs. Throgmorton pressed it into her hand.

"Thank you. I wasn't expecting it to be so chilly tonight. The weather hasn't been that bad yet."

"Did you use the valet parking?" Mrs. Throgmorton asked.

Courtney shook her head. "I didn't feel right, and I wasn't even sure if I should since I'm not a member."

"Nonsense. You're a guest, and that means you should be treated even better than the members. I really am so glad you came, Courtney. I think a night like this could be very good for you and the shelter."

Courtney had thought so, too, when Mrs. Throgmorton had invited her. Now that she was actually here, she just felt inadequate. "I'm not sure. I doubt anybody wants to hear about the shelter."

Mrs. Throgmorton leaned down to scratch Peppa's head. "I know it seems like the wealthy must do nothing but talk of golf and vacationing, but I assure you that isn't the case. Most of us are looking for some way we can give back. It looks good, and it's always a bonus at tax time. Even if you can't persuade anyone with emotions or morals, you can always get them in the pocketbook." She gave Courtney a conspiratorial smile.

"I don't want to take advantage of anyone," Courtney hesitated. She was tempted to stay for just an hour or so and then duck out, claiming that Peppa was getting restless.

"Not at all, and I wouldn't suggest it!" Mrs. Throgmorton countered. "If you're open and honest with them, they'll see the opportunities they're looking for. Let's see." She paused as she looked around the room. "Come with me. I'll introduce you to the Livingstons."

Courtney felt as though everyone at the party was looking at her as Mrs. Throgmorton led her across the room. She knew it was mostly because she had a dog with her, and that didn't usually bother her, but right now she felt like she stood out like a sore thumb. She ran a hand around to the back of her neck to make sure the tag on her dress wasn't hanging out.

"Louis, Natasha, I'd love for you to meet my friend Courtney Cain. She runs the Curly Bay Pet Hotel and Rescue here in town."

"Nice to meet you." Mr. Livingston shook her hand.

Natasha, however, was far more interested in the dog than she was Courtney. Despite her couture dress, she was crouched down to love all over Peppa. "Hello, sweet thing! We never get to see beautiful creatures like yourself in here! How are you? What's your name?"

Courtney was grateful for any chance to talk about Peppa, especially if it meant she didn't have to talk about herself. "This is Peppa."

"Hi, Peppa!" Natasha laughed as the dog licked her face, having little concern for her pearl earrings. "Is she up for adoption?"

"No, I'm afraid she's not. When she came to the shelter, she was terrified of people. I fostered her in my home to get her used to meeting new people and potential adopters. I was already thinking about adopting her myself, and when she saved my life I knew I couldn't live a day without her." Courtney gazed down lovingly at her dog, so grateful that Peppa had come into her life.

"What a good girl!" Natasha enthused. "Louis, we need a dog!"

Her husband rocked back on his heels and stuffed his hands in his pockets. "I don't think we do, dear."

"But they're wonderful protection. You heard what she just said about Peppa saving her life," Natasha protested.

Louis knotted his eyebrows as he looked at Courtney. "Was she trained to do that?"

"No, this was all her own idea. I like to think it was simply because she cares about me. Of course, I would never want to assume that just any dog can be a guard dog. I do know the name of a good trainer, if you ever find yourself in the position." She hesitated. Any dog that was adopted by someone like the Livingstons would no doubt have a good home. They probably had plenty of money to take care of vet bills and proper food, but Courtney didn't want them to adopt a dog under the wrong pretenses.

"Still, it's best to adopt them simply as companions. I think that's really what they're meant for."

"Of course," Natasha cooed, making kissy faces at Peppa. "I could have a sweet little baby like you at home, and when Louis is off at work we could hang out at the pool or go visit my sister. Do you have a friend at the shelter who would like that?"

"If you're interested in coming in to look at some of our adoptable dogs, I'd be more than happy to give you a tour," Courtney offered.

Mrs. Throgmorton, who'd been quiet up until this point, cleared her throat. "It's a shame that there are so many homeless animals who end up at the shelter, you know. They do their best to keep up with funding through their hotel and day spa, but it often isn't enough to cover all the expenses. I often help organize fundraisers."

While the dog itself hadn't sparked Mr. Livingston's interest, this did. "Ah, yes. I remember hearing about one of those last year. I'm afraid I had an out-of-town business meeting and I couldn't attend. Perhaps there's something we can do to help."

Mrs. Throgmorton secretly winked at Courtney.

The rest of the evening went much the same way. Time passed quickly as Mrs. Throgmorton escorted her around the room, introducing her to anyone whom she thought might be interested in hearing more about the shelter. At one point, Courtney spotted Miles Dorrington on the other side of the room, chatting with the other social elite, and she was grateful that Mrs. Throgmorton didn't try to get her to talk to him.

"My dear, I do believe this is going wonderfully," Mrs. Throgmorton gushed when they sat down at one of the tables to have a bite to eat. She'd only put a couple of oysters on her plate alongside a very tiny salad. "You've given your name and number to quite a few people, and I have no doubt that others will be contacting me later to get your information if they didn't already.

"They did seem interested," Courtney admitted as she slipped a bite of prime rib to Peppa. "I just hope their interest was genuine. Whether networking here brings in either adoptions or fundraising, it works for me. Volunteers and fosters would be excellent as well."

"I have no doubt you'll get a little bit of everything," Mrs. Throgmorton noted as she took a sip of champagne. "The only people who don't want dogs must be very cold at heart. You'll probably find quite a few who prefer the independence of a cat. But if you'll excuse me for the moment, I see someone I need to speak to. Do feel free to get dessert when you're ready." She gestured to the dessert table as she excused herself.

Courtney allowed herself to indulge in her meal. She'd loaded her plate down far more than Mrs. Throgmorton had, but then again she didn't have any sort of reputation to keep up with here. She'd taken a little bit of everything from the buffet, finding it all perfectly seasoned, perfectly warmed, and perfectly delicious.

"Let's hit the desserts, Peppa. Maybe we can find a bit of vanilla ice cream or something for you."

The table was practically groaning with sweets. Courtney felt a pang of guilt, thinking once again of that poor woman at the checkout who hadn't been able to pay for her food. She promised herself she'd make some donations to the food pantry as soon as the grocery shelves were full again, and then she began to head down the long line of goodies.

"I'm so glad we're having a party," said a voice nearby as Courtney plucked a tiny square of chocolate cake from a tray with an equally tiny pair of tongs. "I'm already so bored now that the holidays are over."

Courtney looked up. She recognized some of the women who were heading down the dessert table ahead of her, and she knew Mrs. Throgmorton had introduced her to some of them.

"I know, but I do get bored of the same old thing at the country club parties," Mrs. Richmond replied as she took a miniature cheesecake topped with a raspberry. "I prefer house parties."

"Speaking of, did you go to any of Miles Dorrington's parties this year?" This came from Melissa Stanwick, whom Mrs. Throgmorton had pointed out to Courtney but not introduced her to. She'd claimed the Stanwicks weren't the type to make generous donations.

"Every year," Mrs. Chang said as she sampled a handmade bonbon. "Miles always throws the best parties."

"Yes, he always *has,*" Melissa agreed. "I noticed this year that they were incredibly understaffed. I hardly saw anyone coming around to offer drinks and appetizers, and the catering was subpar, to say the least."

"Now that you mention it, the champagne he served on New Year's Eve tasted rather cheap," Mrs. Richmond acknowledged. She took a truffle from a tray and frowned at it, probably wondering what it would do to her waistline.

"I wonder what's going on with him," Mrs. Chang mused. "I did hear something about him not going ahead and remodeling his kitchen as he planned."

Courtney pretended not to listen, but it was impossible when they were all standing right there and gossiping. Even though she knew Mr. Dorrington wasn't pleased with her, Courtney still felt odd about overhearing others talk about him that way. With her plate full, she and Peppa headed back to the table.

CHAPTER NINE

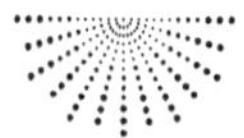

Despite her initial thoughts of leaving early, Courtney found that she'd been so busy at the country club that time had been flying. Before she knew it, she'd stayed the entire evening. She'd only even noticed the late hour when she realized Peppa was snoring, her head on Courtney's one good pair of shoes. "I guess I'd better get going," she said as she checked her watch. It was after eleven. "Thank you so much for inviting me."

"Not at all," Mrs. Throgmorton gushed. "Perhaps you'll consider becoming a member sometime."

"Oh, I'm not sure about that." She didn't even want to ask what the membership fee was, and even if she could afford it, she knew that sort of money probably had better places to go.

"If you do, I'll be happy to sponsor you." The older woman got up from her seat as they walked toward the door. "I should be getting out of here, too. Sir Glitter gets upset with me when I stay gone from the house too long, you know."

"I have no doubt of it."

"If you ladies will give us just a moment, we're working to clear the steps," James said, stepping in front of them before they could get into the foyer.

"Clear them of what?" Mrs. Throgmorton demanded.

"The ice and snow, ma'am. Quite a bit of it has fallen the evening. I've heard reports that the roads are really bad already."

Courtney peeked around him and through the outer set of doors as another young man went through them with a bag of salt under his arm. She could see the blowing whiteness flowing down from the sky, and the blast of chill that came through the door behind him didn't bode well for her trip home. "So it's finally come. All this time, I didn't know whether to believe everybody who kept saying we would have a bad winter storm, and now here it is while I'm away from home and wearing heels."

"Do let the valet get your car this time, dear. They'll clear the windshield for you and everything." Mrs. Throgmorton practically took Courtney's keys from her hand and gave them to James.

When her car was pulled up in front of the building, warmed up and the windshield cleared, Courtney pulled in a deep breath. She didn't want to be out in this weather. Everyone had told her to prepare for it, and she'd been silly enough not to believe them.

"Be careful," Mrs. Throgmorton called as she pulled on her faux fur coat.

"You, too!" Courtney let James help her down the icy steps and into her car, and then she was on her way. She paused at the end of the parking lot where she wouldn't be in the way of the valet retrieving other cars. "I think we should get you buckled in, too, Peppa. It's going to be an interesting ride home."

Peppa was well-trained, and she didn't object as Courtney buckled her into a special harness and then into the seatbelt.

"We're just going to take it slow," she said to herself as she crept out toward the main road. She kept the radio off, just to help her concentrate, but the heaters were blowing at their highest setting. "It's just a little trip across town and then out to our place. I'm sure that the city has at least kept the main roads clear, and it isn't as though I've never driven in the snow before, right?"

Peppa didn't seem to understand the danger of what they were doing. She relaxed into the seat and closed her eyes, enjoying the heat.

Courtney kept the wheel steady, but the ice that had frozen to the road proved to be far more than she could handle. She felt the back end of the car slip out of control first, yanking her toward the ditch. She tried to correct it, but her efforts only made her slide a different way. Like a nightmare she couldn't wake up from, Courtney fought as the car slid straight off the road.

"Are you okay, baby?" She checked over Peppa, who looked alarmed but whole. "Okay. It's just a little ditch. Maybe the grass will give us better traction than the road." She put the car in low gear and slowly feathered the gas pedal, hoping to get back on track, but it was to no avail. They were stuck.

Courtney took her cell out of the tiny clutch she'd brought into the party. "Of course," she groaned as the screen remained stubbornly black. "It's dead. I don't even know if I can charge it with the car. And if I can, it's probably going to take forever." Waves of dread washed over her. It was a long walk back to the country club, especially in heels, and it was far too long of a walk to get all the way home. "I don't know what we're going to do, Peppa."

"Woof!" The dog wasn't listening. Her eyes were focused on the road behind them, and she barked again.

Courtney turned to see headlights on the side of the road behind her, but the vehicle wasn't in the ditch like she was. She rolled her window down to find Miles Dorrington, of all people, standing next to her car.

"Are you all right?" he shouted over the wind.

"Yes, just shaken up a little. I just can't get out of here, and my cell is dead." Courtney wondered if he recognized her. He'd been so angry with her when she'd talked to him on the phone about Lulabelle that she doubted he'd have pulled over if he'd known it was her.

"That's all right. I can give you a ride."

Courtney squinted through the darkness at his big, luxury SUV. "Can I bring my dog?"

"Of course! We're not going to leave her here. Come on. Careful now. Everything is slick."

They slowly made their way back to his SUV. Courtney put Peppa in the backseat before climbing in the front, and she practically melted as she sank into the heated seats. "Thank you so much for stopping. I thought I was a goner for a minute. I'll have to get someone out here to pull it out of the ditch, though."

Miles shook his head. He'd put a thick woolen overcoat over the suit he'd worn for the evening, but a rather incongruous beanie had been pulled down over his white hair. "There's no point in doing it tonight," he said as he put his SUV in gear. "I've been listening to the scanner, and there are cars off the road everywhere. The police have asked everyone to stay put unless it's an emergency, because even they are having a hard time getting around. You don't have any hope of a tow truck tonight."

"I guess you're right. It can wait until morning." She watched as they headed slowly down the road, leaving her car behind in the darkness. "I live all the way on the other side of town on Mahogany road, though. I don't want you to put yourself out just to get me there."

"It's not a problem," he reassured her. "This big clunker is horrible on gas, but it's too heavy to slide off the road. Besides, it's not as though I'm just going to drop you off in the middle of town and leave you there."

"I really do appreciate it," she replied. She studied the dashboard, looking for something else to say. "It was a really nice party."

"Yes, I saw you making your rounds. Everyone seemed quite enchanted with you and your dog. Leave it to Mrs. Throgmorton to get those stuffed shirts to say yes to having an animal on the premises," he said with a laugh. "I could march in there with Lulabelle tomorrow and they'd probably throw me out of the club!"

"I thought they were going to throw me back out on my ear when I showed up at the door," Courtney admitted. "Everyone was actually really nice, though."

"Nicer than I've been to you." Miles adjusted the collar of his coat as he made the next turn. "Not that I'm glad you slid off the road, but I am glad to have the chance to talk to you in private. I was very rude to you last week on the phone."

"Oh, it's all right."

"No, it's not," he insisted. "I was very impolite, and I accused Dora of not doing her job. I imagine she wasn't very happy about that."

"Well, no," Courtney admitted. "Was her hair really that short? I would like a chance to fix whatever we did wrong."

Mr. Dorrington pulled in a deep breath. His silvery brows furrowed, and he looked like he was really concentrating. "No. What actually happened is that I was having a bad day. You see, I'm a silent partner in several companies. I have a lot I'm dealing with financially, and in a panic I realized I needed to find some ways to cut corners. I didn't want to just tell you I couldn't afford to have Lulabelle groomed regularly, and so I took it out on you ladies instead of just being honest. I really am sorry."

"That's all right. Peppa, stop." Courtney noticed Peppa was digging around under the back seat, and the last thing she needed was for her big, silly mutt to tear up the carpeting in Mr. Dorrington's vehicle. "I promise you, we would've understood."

"I know that now. I'll schedule a new appointment soon."

"Peppa, stop!" Courtney reached further into the backseat. She tugged at Peppa's collar, but the dog was unrelenting.

"What's she doing?" Miles asked.

"Getting into something, it looks like. I'm so sorry. She's not usually like this." Courtney twisted in the big leather seat, fighting with the arm rest so she could reach all the way into the back to stop whatever Peppa was doing. Of all the times for her to get herself into trouble, this wasn't it. Mr. Dorrington had apologized, and he was going to bring Lulabelle back for a grooming appointment at some point, and she didn't want all of that to go down the drain just because Peppa was bored and wanted to dig around.

Courtney managed to get her fingers around Peppa's collar. The dog had her head buried under the seat, and Courtney couldn't see what she was after in the darkness, so she pulled back. Peppa had the corner of a red checkered blanket in her mouth. It was smeared with dirt and blood. Courtney's heart dropped into her stomach, and her stomach dropped into her feet. "What the heck?"

The plastic bag that Peppa had found also contained some ratty old clothes. Courtney had only seen them once before, but she knew exactly where she'd seen them. "What's going on, Mr. Dorrington?"

Miles slammed his palm against the steering wheel. "Leave it to a stupid dog to figure it all out," he grumbled as he pressed the gas pedal.

The car was moving too quickly for conditions, and Courtney was starting to get scared. "Slow down! Please! We don't want to end up in the ditch again!"

"In the ditch is exactly where I've been when it comes to money," he said, hardly seeming to notice that the back tires were skidding slightly on the slick road. "I tried to fix it, and I was on my way to making things better, but everyone else seems to have other plans for me, don't they?"

"Mr. Dorrington, maybe you should just pull over and let me out here," Courtney said. She'd let go of Peppa for the moment and was gripping the arm rest. She didn't know why Miles had the items from the park, but she didn't like it.

"See, nobody thinks that a wealthy man will ever lose his fortune, not one that he's spent decades building up. I was always very careful with my money, you know. But a few bad investments, a few partnerships in companies that didn't take off the way I thought they would, and all of a sudden everyone is talking about me. So I didn't serve the best champaign on New Year's Eve. So I'm not going to be vacation in the Bahamas this year. Is that so bad?"

"No. Of course not," Courtney said, mostly because she felt as though she had to reply somehow. But she'd also overheard the gossip at the country club, and she knew the answer was different for Miles.

"I shouldn't have taken the money from the donation box, but it was all right there in front of me. Nobody was even watching it. I've done a few questionable things with some of my investments, but I've never outright stolen anything. I thought I could get away with it, and some good Samaritan would come along and replace it for the shelter," Miles continued. "It was a harmless crime. Until Glenn saw me, the miserable coot."

They were heading into the city limits now, but Mr. Dorrington wasn't slowing down like he should be. She was terrified, but she had to know the truth. "So you killed him? And the man sleeping in the park?"

Miles let out a snort of a laugh. "You're pretty oblivious. Even I know that Glenn was sleeping in the park. He'd lost his home and everything else he had. The last thing I wanted was to end up like him, and if committing a small crime or two would keep my head afloat, then so be it. But like I said, Glenn saw me. He stopped me in the park the night after your little signup event, and he told me he'd give me twenty-four hours to confess before he turned me in. Well, I couldn't exactly let the public know what I'd done. Not at any cost."

It all made sense now, but in a horrible way that Courtney didn't want to think about. "Stop the car. Let me out."

"I can't do that," he replied, far too calmly. "I had to get rid of Glenn, and now I'll have to get rid of you, too." Miles pressed his foot down harder on the gas pedal.

Feeling desperate, Courtney reached across the console for the steering wheel. She didn't know what her plan was, but her situation felt hopeless if she just let him do whatever he wanted. Miles slapped at her hands to get them off the wheel, pulling just as hard to the left as she was pulling to the right.

Peppa let out a bark of warning.

"Just pull over!" Courtney screamed. "Let us out!"

"No!" Mr. Dorrington smacked at her arms and hands once again.

Peppa wasn't about to put up with it. She leapt into the front seat and sank her teeth in Mr. Dorrington's shoulder. The man screamed and let go of the steering wheel. Courtney yanked it to the right, and the car veered dangerously. Courtney tried to straighten it out, but she had no control over the gas or the brakes. Pulling in a breath, she yanked the wheel as hard and fast to the right as she could. The tires bumped up over the sidewalk. Ice and snow slipped perilously underneath the tread as the SUV skidded sideways through a parking lot and into a utility pole.

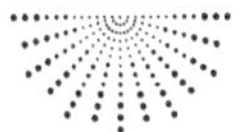

CHAPTER TEN

The volunteers were coming in right on time. Courtney had spent the entire morning setting up, but she'd been worried all day that things wouldn't go as planned. Nothing really had over the last couple of weeks, and even though the worst of it had all been resolved, she found herself feeling a little jumpy.

"Okay," Lisa said as she came out of the children's room at the library. "I used all the bean bag chairs and rugs we have to make separate spaces for everyone, and there's plenty of space in the other rooms as well. Those extra blankets you brought are really going to come in handy."

"Wonderful. I've got all the paperwork ready to go. I usually keep it all printed out and ready to go, but I'd gotten a little behind on it." She glanced at the stacks of paperwork that were arranged on a table near the circulation desk. There were waivers for new volunteers to sign, as well as adoption applications for anyone who found themselves in love with the pup they'd come in to read to.

"That's understandable. Are you feeling okay?" Lisa asked, her brow wrinkling in concern.

"Oh, yeah. I'm fine." And she was, mostly. It was hard not to think about the night of the country club party every time she got behind the wheel of her car, which fortunately had been rescued from the ditch without any harm. The impact of that utility pole still left her shoulder aching sometimes, but she was grateful that she and Peppa had both walked away unharmed. Actually, it was more like they ran away as fast as they could.

Courtney's feet had crunched through ice-coated grass, her chilled hands hanging on to Peppa's leash as they sprinted across several yards. She'd been fortunate that Peppa hadn't found Glenn's belongings until they were nearly into town, or else she might've had to go for miles before she found someone with their porch light on. Courtney had run straight up onto the steps of a cozy-looking brick house, slamming on the door and screaming for help. She felt bad for the poor woman she'd disturbed, who was just as scared as Courtney was when she'd found out what was happening.

"And I suppose Dora and Jessi will be along with the dogs soon? Or are you supposed to go back and get them?" Lisa asked, bringing Courtney back to the present moment.

She was grateful for that, considering that it wasn't a good idea to swim around in such awful memories for long. Courtney knew that she would never really forget the way that Miles had so cold-heartedly explained his reasoning for killing Glenn, and she would probably think about Glenn and other homeless people every time she went to the grocery store or the weather turned cold, but at least she knew she was doing everything she could to help. Her first big donation to the food pantry had already been dropped off.

"Yes. It's not a good thing that our shelter is full right now, but we do have plenty of dogs to match up with the volunteers. With a little luck, there will be fewer of them staying at the shelter by the end of the week. I'll send Jessi a text to let her know the volunteers are showing up. We didn't want to bring any of the animals in too early."

"Do you need to charge your phone while you're here?" Lisa offered.

"Nope. I finally got myself a shiny new one." Courtney held up the device as proof. "I hardly know how to use it, since everything is in a different place, but at least the battery actually works and I can charge it. I should've done this a long time ago."

Lisa made a face. "I agree with that, but I won't say I told you so."

"That's okay. Everyone else did."

As the volunteers filed into the lobby, Courtney directed them to the conference room. "Ladies and gentlemen, I'm so glad you could be here with us today. I know that this event didn't happen on the day that we planned, due to that nasty winter storm, but I'm so grateful that you could still come out and join us today while the sun is shining." All the ice and snow had been cleared from the roads, and even though it still occupied a few rooftops and shady yards, Curly Bay was looking a lot more like the little town she'd gotten so used to over the last six months or so. "You'll each be assigned a dog as they come in. We have a couple of different rooms with some comfortable spaces set up on the floor. We'll be here for about an hour, and if you or the dog have any problems, you can come find one of us. There will be refreshments afterwards. Are there any questions?"

A little girl who'd come in with her mom raised her hand. Courtney instantly recognized her as Sophie, the little girl from story hour who had been so concerned about whether or not Shelby had a home. "Is Shelby here?"

Courtney smiled, and it was hard not to give anything away due to just how excited she was. Sophie had given her mother the shelter's contact information, and the two of them had talked for quite some time over the phone. Mrs. Conrad had even come into the shelter to meet Shelby for herself, and she'd fallen just as in love as her daughter had. "She certainly is, and she tells me she would love for you to read some books to her today."

Sophie's big blue eyes got even bigger as she clapped with joy.

The dogs arrived, and the volunteers split off into various areas to curl up with their pups. Everyone from children with their parents to affluent businesspeople were sitting on the floor. They were reading books, magazines, and even technical manuals. Alex Strickland had come through on his promise to read about home construction, but the old basset mix that he sat next to didn't seem to mind a bit.

"Everything is going well," Lisa whispered as everyone got settled. "Can you believe what a great job Nora did of setting up the refreshments?"

Courtney had taken a peek earlier. When Nora had volunteered to help, she really only needed to set out the box of cookies and some cups of punch. But she'd covered the table with a fancy cloth, found little paper doilies to set out the treats, and had even added a pan of brownies that she'd made herself. "I think maybe she feels a little guilty for the way she was treating everyone. None of us had any clue that Glenn was so down on his luck. The divorce and the alimony payments had put him behind, and then he'd had court fees when he had that land dispute with Alex. It all just added up over time. I only wish that he'd reached out for help."

"Me, too," Lisa agreed. "Is there anything else you need me to do?"

"Yes. Just look right over there." Courtney pointed to a large bean bag chair just inside the children's room. Sophie and Shelby were both curled up on it, and Mrs. Conrad sat next to them on the floor. The dog was so happy to have this little girl reading to her, and her tail constantly swished against the floor.

"I think Shelby really likes you," Mrs. Conrad said.

"I like her, too." Sophie put the book down for a moment so she could pet Shelby behind the ears and kiss her head. "I just feel really bad that she doesn't have a home."

Mrs. Conrad nodded. "I know. I was thinking about that. Maybe we should give her a home."

Sophie's hands stopped in Shelby's deep golden fur as she stared at her mother. "Do you mean…?"

"Yes. I've already talked with Courtney and filled out all the paperwork. As soon as we're done here today, Shelby can come straight home with us."

Sophie's scream could be heard all over the library, but Courtney knew nobody would mind if they could see the joy on the little girl's face as she launched out of the bean bag chair and into her mother's arms. Shelby joined the pile on the floor as they all hugged and kissed and laughed.

Courtney wiped a tear from the corner of her eye. "That's what it's all about."

THANK YOU FOR CHOOSING A PUREREAD BOOK!

We hope you enjoyed the story, and as a way to thank you for choosing PureRead we'd like to send you this free Special Edition Cozy, and other fun reader rewards…

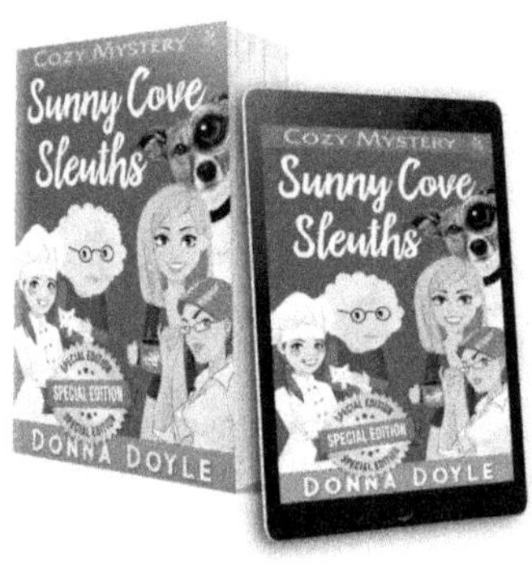

Click Here to download your free Cozy Mystery
PureRead.com/cozy

Thanks again for reading.

See you soon!

At PureRead we publish books you can trust. Great tales without smut or swearing, but with all of the mystery and romance you expect from a great story.

Be the first to know when we release new books, take part in our fun competitions, and get surprise free books in your inbox by signing up to our Reader list.

As a thank you you'll receive this exclusive Special Edition Cozy available only to our subscribers...

Click Here to download your free Cozy Mystery
PureRead.com/cozy

Thanks again for reading.
See you soon!